"Will you dance with me, Sylvie?"

"You know she can't do that," Achille said, a little sternly. "She hasn't decided."

"Sure she has. Did you really have a choice, Sylvie? Would you go back to your old life now, after what you've learned?"

In one quick motion that took her off guard, Lucien pulled Sylvie to her feet and held her close. "Even now," he whispered to her, "you feel the excitement out here on the bayou, the flow of power, the sexual tension that we all feel on nights like this. You can't lie to me. Of all of us here, I know you better than you know yourself."

Without a trace of shyness or reluctance, and oblivious of Achille's slight scowl, he swept Sylvie up into a long, hot kiss that made her dizzy.

"The werewolf's kiss," he said, leaning over to brush his lips seductively over her ear as he spoke. "When the time comes, make sure I'm the one."

✝

"SCOTCH DOES FOR WEREWOLVES WHAT ANNE RICE DID FOR VAMPIRES. In this multi-generational saga of lycanthropy, the werewolf leaps into the 1990s. Settle in for a well-written, e_____."
—JOSEPH_____

"DRAWS THE READ_____
BRACE . . . Keep your_____
reigning queen of chi_____
—RA_____